ADLEY'S FARM

Kana Ugess

Adley's Farm
by Kana Ugess

This is a work of fiction. Names, characters,
places, and incidents either are the product
of the author's imagination or are used
fictitiously. Any resemblance to actual
persons, living or dead, events, or locales is
entirely coincidental.

First paperback edition 2021

Dedication:

For anyone suffering with or knows someone suffering with ME.

Table of Contents

Acknowledgements

I would like to thank my unwitting volunteers who didn't know I had written a book highlighting their chronic symptoms until I asked them to be beta readers. This is for you, Uncle Ben, as I watched you have to give up the chickens, ducks and all other birds on the farm. For my cousin, Jenny, because you have had your late teens and consequent adulthood robbed by this disease. For a dear friend, Rea, who is always full of good humour and ready to be there for my family and me, despite your own battle with ME.

A special thanks to my mother, who is always the first to read my work, and I undoubtedly believe she is my biggest fan. And to my dad, whose farm knowledge has been invaluable.

To everyone who has helped me get this far, thank you.

1

Arthur smiled softly at the ducks in front of him. Most were bobbing on the pond with easy-going quacks of contentment. He, on the other hand, was feeling deflated.

"I don't think they're ever going to find out what's wrong with me, Jess." With a solemn sigh, he patted the Border Collie's head as she sat at his feet. She looked up at him with her rich brown eyes before returning her gaze to the ducks.

"Every time I have to leave here to be poked and prodded, not to mention the same circle of questions, is time lost looking after this lot," he complained, waving an arm exaggeratedly at the land sprawling behind him. "It's just a complete waste of time!"

Jess whined a little and leaned against his leg.

Arthur rested his hand on her head, crouching down slowly as his joints complained at the action. "I know; you're right as always."

She licked his nose, then, as Arthur pulled away slightly, she flicked her tongue out several times; flashes of pink appeared around her lips, all the while, her eyes staring deep into his.

"Alright, I promise I will keep my appointment with Harry... see what the doctor orders this time, hey Jess?"

Unfolding himself with a groan, he threw the last handful of feed on the shore of the pond, much to the ducks' excitement. Leaving soft quacks of appreciation behind him, he started to make his way back towards the farmhouse.

Even from this far away, the state of the farmhouse pulled at his heartstrings. The gutter was clearly coming away, and on closer inspection, you could see the water stains caused by it, clearly marking the wall in a mossy green hue. The window sills were cracked and flaking in their once proud black paint, not to mention how shabby the rendering was looking. Even the end wall was completely overgrown with ivy; he just couldn't muster the strength to pull it away. In any case, as soon as he did, it would grow back again.

Disheartened, he brought his gaze away to the small orchard that grew beside the paddock. Then he caught sight of the patch of land that used to be a vegetable patch. Tall grasses and nettles now made that area their home. He closed his eyes briefly with a sigh.

Wistfully, he observed the geese and chickens. He had contemplated for at least the last four months about the future of these birds.

The chickens were, on the one hand, major egg providers and a part of his daily income. There were five wooden hen houses with nest boxes on either side. During the day, they had full access to the entire field he had converted into one large coop, with the help of some aviary panels to deter predators. But it was clearly becoming too much work for his ailing body to keep up with the cleaning as regularly as he should; it was back-breaking work.

The geese, on the other hand, were noisy and temperamental, though they kept the grass in the field neighbouring the chickens in check. As loud as they were, they mostly looked after themselves, and it didn't matter if it rained. But ensuring the fifty or so geese were locked away back in the goose huts at night was a taxing job - especially on his worsening bad days where his muscles screamed, and exhaustion weighed him down.

Jess helped massively when it came to putting the birds away, it had become a private joke between the farmer and his dog that she was a fowl dog instead of a sheepdog. Though it was apparent to Arthur that, even with her help, if he couldn't determine what was causing his symptoms, their income would disappear, along with their ability to run Adley's Farm.

Ambling down the side of the pigsty, he heard his two Gloucester Old Spots, Rosie and Pippin, grunting merrily to themselves. He reached the far field that doubled up as a paddock for Toby, his black Shire horse and the two Jersey cows, Bessie and Maisie.

Toby was always pleased to see him and plodded his way across to the fence where Arthur gave the white blaze on his nose a stroke; then, with a farewell pat on the neck, he continued round to the courtyard.

Ensuring the milk churns and remaining fresh eggs were placed by the gate ready for collection, Arthur disappeared into the farmhouse, Jess at his heels.

The front door opened straight into the kitchen, the centrepiece of which was the traditional farmhouse table. Jess's bed was down here, too, particularly on the colder nights where Arthur dragged it in front of the range.

He continued through the next door into the study, bypassing the stairs. The study was his favourite room. Except for the writing desk that stood next to the gun cabinet on the wall against the kitchen, the room was full of bookshelves. His books had always maintained a special place in his heart; it was the only way he could truly relax. From Shakespeare to Dickens and Hardy to Twain, the shelves were colourful and dust-free. His armchair stood in front of the gun cabinet, placed so he could watch the chickens from his window when he wasn't reading.

Still walking through the downstairs, he came to the living room. A large Georgian fireplace with an open hearth was the focal point against the far wall, a sofa facing towards it and a long sideboard dresser against the wall just as you came in.

It was this dresser he aimed for. Upon it stood a fading photo of a smiling woman and a young boy. Just in front of this lay his keys to the Land Rover.

Jess's tail began to wag as she saw him pick the keys up; she gave an agreeable bark.

Arthur smiled at her before making his way back outside. "I'm going before I talk myself out of it again."

Jess barked once more, trotting after Arthur.

"You're in charge!" he called through the open driver's window as he pulled away.

2

"Oh Jess," Arthur sighed, patting the soft furry head that appeared over the fence as he approached. "I'm glad to see your face, girl." With another sigh, he pushed open the gate.

Jess was already at his side sniffing his boots.

"I couldn't hide a mistress from you, could I?" he declared, chuckling quietly to himself. "Now away with you before you send me flying."

Jess obediently ran away from his side but, when he didn't follow, she came back. Arthur steeled himself, staring straight ahead at the farmhouse and placing one foot in front of the other. He gritted his teeth against the pain and continued to force forward. Jess followed by his side, ever mindful not to get too close.

Finally reaching the courtyard, Arthur lamented at the brief walk from the garage. It had been an addition during his grandfather's time, and due to the layout of the farm, it had been built behind the barn that housed the tractor and other machinery. He scoffed at the memory of his grandfather's voice as he proudly announced this building's completion. How little did he appreciate as a child that having to walk even that short distance would one day be a great challenge to himself. It was ridiculous.

He glanced down at Jess, her tail wagging slightly as he reached down to pat her head. "Well, we made it." He tried to smile down at her brown eyes as she gazed longingly up at him, leaning into his leg gently. "I'm afraid, Jess, if I stop, I won't be able to carry on." He sighed determinedly, "Right then, let's get them all to bed, then sort ourselves out, hey girl?"

With one final pat, Jess left his side again and ran towards the barn. Arthur followed slowly, grabbing the buckets of feed, his nerves burning at the touch, and placing them in the wheelbarrow. He winced at the pain as he bent down to pick up the handles; then, with a groan, he carried on, pushing all thoughts to the back of his mind that weren't focused on his animals.

First, he checked on the pigs, Toby and the cows. He was somewhat glad when it came to milking time as he sat down and rested his head against the cow's flank. Though, begrudgingly, he admitted he was beginning to wish he hadn't sat down at all. He dragged the milk churns on a sack truck to the side gate ready for collection tomorrow and then headed out into the fields.

Heading to the chicken coop where all the hen houses stood, he found some had already started heading indoors to roost. He checked all their water feeders then, with a quick whistle, Jess was rounding them up, and it wasn't long before he had locked all the doors for the night.

The geese put up more of a fight, but they too were soon locked away safe until the morning, and he had managed to pocket another two eggs from them.

Finally, he made his way to the pond, where his pride and joy stayed. The ducks were always good at putting themselves to bed. He smiled at their soft whispering quacks of goodnight as he shut the door.

Hobbling to turn around, he caught sight of Jess lying in the grass watching him. "What say you, dinner time?" He smiled as he watched her tail wag enthusiastically. "Alright, alright, I'm getting there."

Jess shot off back towards the farmhouse, and with a sigh, Arthur slowly followed. He smiled weakly when Jess reappeared and walked beside him.

He screwed his face up in pain as he pulled his wellies off, though grateful for the sheepskin slippers that helped to warm his toes a little afterwards.

Once in the kitchen, he flicked the switch for the kettle and poured Jess her dinner before collapsing in his chair. Feeling the cold creeping along his bones, he pulled a blanket over his legs and hugged his body with his arms. Jess trotted in, sitting with her head resting on his thigh.

"Jess, my girl," he sighed, placing a weathered hand on her head and fondling her soft ears. "I went to the surgery to see Harry today like I said I would, but it's not good." He glanced out of the window beside him, "he said I've got Myalgic Encephalopathy[1] or something or other. It's not good, Jess, it's not good."

Overcome with mind-numbing exhaustion and wracked with pain, Arthur allowed himself to succumb to sleep. The kettle boiled with a click; Jess trotted to the kitchen, expecting Arthur to follow. She turned to see him lying motionless with soft breaths, returned to his side and licked his hand before curling up on the floor at his feet.

---

[1] Please take a look at the end of the book for more information on Myalgic Encephalopathy - ME.

3

A month had passed where Arthur had remained steadfast in his duties to his animals. He was determined that, at any cost, they would always come first. On the bad days, he found that going back to bed, waking again in time for the evening rounds, then once again entrenching himself within the land of nod was far preferable than forcing himself to carry on all day. Meanwhile, though he tried to be more productive on the good days, he always found it came at a cost. For every minute he pushed himself further, it felt like it would take an hour or more to recover from the physical fatigue and overwhelming pain that followed. So, he took to ensuring the essential jobs for that day were done before sitting with a book until the animals required him again.

Jess had adapted too, becoming a gentle reminder to him when he hadn't responded to his alarms, nudging her nose in his hands or licking his face until he came to. Other times she led the way around the farm; he wouldn't admit it to anyone else, but he was grateful to her when he had forgotten what he was going to do next. She was always there to remind and guide him to the next job. She was always there to comfort him when he became frustrated at himself for forgetting.

Together they maintained the farm, making sure all animals were fed, living clean and healthily, the eggs were collected, and the milk churns were left out, ready to be picked up every day. It was hard work but tougher still when the pain travelled throughout his body. His legs could buckle under sheer exhaustion before he had even climbed out of bed or from the sofa if he hadn't been able to face the stairs the night before.

A ringing in his ears and the sun's warmth on his face slowly brought him around from his slumber. Confused, he tried to locate where the noise was coming from. Jess was lying on the floor by the door watching him intently, her ears twitching in alert anticipation. She began to wag her tail as he sat up. Leaning over, he picked up the alarm clock from the floor; he had crashed on the sofa last night. Turning the alarm off stopped the hammer, but the ringing in his ears still reverberated through his skull. His head was pounding. An occurrence that was becoming all too familiar a part of his daily routine.

Jess was stood now, doing a dance between Arthur and the door. Her little urgent and almost excitable barks made Arthur instinctively opened the door with his free hand. He followed her to the front door, where she was pawing to be let out. As soon as it was unlocked, she darted off around the corner.

"It's bright this morning," Arthur grumbled through a groggy voice, pinching his nose at the eyes and taking a deep breath. He slowly brought the alarm clock, still in his hand, up to his face and squinted through non-spectacled eyes. "What?"

He turned behind him to check the kitchen clock before once again looking at the clock in his hands. He dashed back to the living room and threw the alarm clock on the sofa, grabbing at his clothes and hastily trying to put them on as he made his way back to the front door. He ignored the screams of anguish his body was putting him through, his fingers shaking as he attempted to finish buttoning up his shirt.

Jess was waiting at the door for him; she glanced at him knowingly before turning sharply on her heels and scurrying to the barn.

Arthur followed in hot pursuit. "Oh Jess, what a fine mess today is turning out to be. How'd it get to be noon already?"

Jess barked in reply with a quick wag of her tail before running back out into the courtyard.

Arthur threw the pig slop down over the wall and into the trough as he rushed out to tend to the chickens. He opened all the hen houses and scattered some corn as flustered feathers flew out into the sunshine. The geese were more aggressively vocal about the delay to which Arthur found himself apologising to them. But it wasn't long before the gaggle forgot the misdemeanour and were waddling away to find a patch of grassland to nibble at. The ducks were rather more passive as they toddled down their ramp with a splash into the pond.

Back in the courtyard, Arthur checked on Toby out in the paddock, offering a carrot in apology, which was appreciatively accepted. Next, he visited the cows. Bessie and Maisie were pleased to finally see him as he threw hay into the wall mangers. Milking was relatively trouble-free, though this afternoon's rushed endeavours were taking their toll on his body.

Jess sat at the byre door panting; she cocked her head to one side as she watched Arthur. When he finished milking, he looked up and smiled weakly at her. "Come on, Jess, let's get you some food too. Heavens knows you deserve it." He left the door to the paddock open for the cows to wander out when they were ready and made his way back to the farmhouse.

Jess sat obediently as she waited for him to pour her food into her bowl. He placed it down gently in front of her with a small smile and stroked her head once, before heading to his chair. She watched him head into the other room before she began to eat, but as soon as she had finished, she then followed after him.

Arthur had collapsed in his armchair, leaning forward with his head in his hands, quiet sobs gently uttering from his quivering lips. Jess sat in front of him and poked her nose between his hands, caringly licking his nose and tear-stained face.

"Not after you've just eaten, Jess," he half chuckled, wiping a hand over his face, "Oh Jess, what are we going to do? I don't know what happened." He hung his head, resting his forehead against hers, ruffling the fur at her shoulders up to her ears. "Well, I think I know what happened, but I don't like what it means, Jess."

She licked her nose and gently pawed at the air in front of her.

Arthur caught the paw with a hand and made a big fuss behind her ears with the other. "I know, I know, I need to talk to Harry again. I promise I'll call him later after practice shuts. I don't want to just be another patient, not when I need a friend," he kissed her nose, "besides you, that is."

4

"Harry."

"Ah, Arthur, I was just thinking about you."

"Oh?"

"I've been making some enquiries. There's a pain clinic-"

"No!"

"Arthur, please?"

"No, I can't be away from here unnecessarily."

Arthur sighed. Leaning against the kitchen worktop, he glanced out of the window at the hen houses; the chickens were milling around in the late afternoon sun. He brought his gaze back inside and caught Jess staring up at him from where she was lying on the floor. She lowered her head back down onto her paws and blinked up at him. The corner of his mouth twitched almost into a half-smile.

"Arthur? Arthur! Are you still there? Hello?" Harry's voice interrupted Arthur's reverie.

"Sorry, Harry."

"You didn't hear a word I was saying, did you?"

"No, sorry," he rubbed a calloused hand against the back of his neck. "Look Harry, can you come over at some point?"

"Sure thing, is everything alright? I can come round now."

Arthur threw a glance at Jess, whose pink tongue reached up to lick her own nose in response. "If you could, that would be great, thank you."

"I'll be with you within the hour."

Arthur placed the phone back on its base. Jess stretched and, with a yawn, came to sit at his feet. "Well then," he patted the top of her head softly, "we best start putting to bed before Harry gets here."

With a small, agreeable bark, Jess led the way back into the courtyard. Arthur ambled after her; it took all his strength to focus on putting one foot in front of the other. They made their way to the geese and chickens. With Jess's herding ability, they were soon all rounded up, and the doors locked for the night. The ducks had once again already settled down, so there wasn't much else for Arthur to do other than bid them goodnight and lock the door.

"Good girl, Jess," he remarked, patting her side before sending her on her way again. She ran only so far before trotting back to his side. She repeated this several times until eventually, they were at the paddock.

Toby hung his head over the fence in greeting.

Arthur reached out and placed a hand against his nose, reaching up and patting his neck with his other hand. "Hello, Toby, old boy." He stood for a short while, alternating his weight from foot to foot slowly as he summoned up the will to persevere.

Bessie and Maisie were ready to come in as Arthur left Toby. In fact, they had already taken themselves into their byre and were helping themselves to any remaining leftovers of their breakfast. Jess ran towards him, her tail wagging, and with a quick bark, disappeared again. Arthur pulled the door closed, topped up the hay levels and left through the door into the courtyard.

Harry was sat on a bench against the farmhouse wall enjoying the last rays of sunlight, his eyes closed and hands clasped over his slightly rotund frame. Jess was sat by the end of the bench watching the byre door. When Arthur appeared, she padded across to him, head low and tail still wagging. Circling behind him, she trotted just ahead until she reached the bench again. She jumped up with both paws resting beside Harry's leg and gave a hushed bark with a dramatic throw back of her head.

"I didn't ask you here to sleep," Arthur declared, nudging Jess away and sitting down with a huff.

"Well, you should have; this spot is just right."

"You can thank Mary for that. She used to sit out here with her crochet." He chuckled softly. "She damn near broke me dragging this bench around until finally, she decided here was the best place."

"Well, she always did like everything in its place. It's a shame she's not here; she knew how to handle you too."

Arthur looked down into his hands, gently twisting the wedding band around his finger. Jess nudged her nose from under his hands and sat between his legs, dumping her head into his lap. He gave a feeble smile as he smoothed her fur back behind her ears.

"Anyway, Harry, the morning I've had… well, the afternoon I've had… it wasn't good."

"What happened?" Harry straightened his back and observed his friend.

"I must've been so exhausted. I couldn't even make it upstairs last night. Even Jess here couldn't wake me like she usually does. The poor girl was waiting to go do her business all morning… I eventually woke up at noon," he fondled Jess's ear absentmindedly.

"Well, you must have needed it. The body does tell us what it needs."

"This isn't normal; what it's telling me is dangerous."

"You can't force yourself."

"It isn't good for the animals, Hal. I'm lucky that today the only issue was being scolded by the fowl!"

Harry remained quiet for a while, mulling it over. "Then maybe it's time to consider packing it all in. You've had a good run, especially on your own but, maybe it's time to look after yourself."

He placed a reassuring hand on Arthur's shoulder. "Not just for you but the animals' welfare too."

"I came to the same conclusion," Arthur sighed, his eyes stinging at holding back tears, "So that's why I'm starting with this." He reached into his shirt pocket and pulled out his glasses case. Upon opening, he shifted his pen and glasses to one side and removed a scrap of paper, handing it to Harry. "If you could do the honours and get this into the newspaper for me, I'd be grateful."

Harry unfolded the paper to see the almost illegible scribbles on the page, "You're going to sell Toby?"

"The old boy needs a good retirement home; I don't want him to go, but I can't risk his health if I have another episode like today. The poultry will go at Christmas like usual, and I just won't replace them. At the moment, the pigs eat the scraps, and the dairy cows make a small income, so we'll see." He leaned forward and picked Jess's head up in his cupped hand, gently stroking her muzzle. "I hate it more than anyone else could, but the animals have to come first."

Harry nodded in silent agreement, disheartened at his friend's current state of affairs. "Right then," he slapped his hands against his knees and stood up. "I best be going. I'll call when it's done."

"Thanks, Hal."

"Hey," Harry paused, "if you ever need me, you know where I am. Jeannie would be happy to have you round for dinner anytime. I'll even come pick you up."

"Thanks for the offer," Arthur rose, folding his case and placing it in his shirt pocket again. "Take some eggs with you before you go. A present for Jeannie."

"She'll appreciate that with all the cake baking she's been doing recently," Harry laughed as Arthur disappeared into the barn and returned with a small punnet of straw cradling a handful of eggs.

Arthur hobbled as far as the paddock as he watched Harry wave goodbye. Toby poked his head over the gate, and Arthur gave his nose a rub. Reaching down into his pocket, he pulled out a strong mint and waited as Toby happily crunched his way through the treat. "Goodnight, old boy," Arthur muttered solemnly as, with a final pat on Toby's neck, he turned to head back into the farmhouse.

5

Staring out at the autumn leaves scattered haphazardly across the lawn, Arthur pulled the blanket up closer to his chin. He ached all over, there was no getting used to the pain, and his headache had been pounding for at least the last hour now. Exhaustion washed over him in waves mixed with nausea forcing him to close his eyes once again.

Painted on the back of his eyelids was a nightmare. A barren wasteland of a farm, eerily silent, apart from the wind whipping around his frail figure. He tried calling out to Jess, but she didn't come; his voice was hoarse, and his throat sore. He turned, hoping to find her by the coop, but there was no chatter from the chickens as they scratched away at the ground. No fluffing and preening of feathers in dust baths. Just a desolate cluster of hen houses; their doors open to dark empty chambers within.

In desperation, he called for Jess over and over again. He searched the goose houses, but they too were silent and looked derelict. The duck house was no longer by the pond; he twisted this way and that, searching for any sign of life. Not a quack, cheep or flapping of wings could be heard. More importantly, there was no Jess.

He woke with a start as pressure increased on his thigh sending shockwaves of pain rippling along his nerves.

"No, Jess," he whispered, gently lifting her head from where she had rested it on his leg. "Oh, my good girl, I know you were worried. Don't look at me like that." He winced as he leaned forward and stroked her fur, placing a gentle kiss on top of her muzzle. "I'm alright, Jess."

Jess's big brown eyes stared soulfully at him, her eyebrows animated in response to his voice. When she seemed convinced that he really was alright, she wagged her tail slowly from side to side, her pink tongue flicking out now and then as she licked her lips.

He stood shakily, wrapping the blanket over his shoulders and hugging himself tightly, the fabric balled in his fists. He shuffled his sheepskin-slipper clad feet across the flagstones and slowly inched his way to the living room, turning off the light as he went. Jess followed obediently, curling herself up on the rug between the fire and sofa. Arthur collapsed onto the sofa, dragging a second blanket off the back cushions and haphazardly throwing it to cover his feet before drawing the remaining over his shoulders, pinning it tightly against him where ever he could.

The fullness of his bladder stirred him from his slumber. Groggily, he tried to throw the blankets aside but gave up with a dejected exhale of breath as the aching in his legs reminded him why he didn't want to get up. He sighed, fighting to open his eyes against the fatigue that clung to him, eventually rolling his head to one side and looking at Jess. She stared back from where she was lying on the floor, her head held high in expectation of movement, her ears alert.

"Can't you go for me, hey?" He mumbled before, with a groan, he urged himself to sit up. Jess blinked in reply and stretched herself before sitting down, all the while still watching him. Arthur took a deep breath and, with an aching moan, finally stood up, using the arm of the sofa to brace his weight. Jess stretched herself again and, with an enthusiastic tail, followed him to the door.

"Alright, you can go out first," Arthur chuckled quietly. Following the wall with his hand for support, he made his way to the front door. Jess shot out, disappearing into the darkness. Arthur closed the door again and braved himself to face the stairs, willing his legs to keep moving.

Climbing the stairs was one thing, but just the thought of coming down was nauseating. He eventually decided that sitting down and descending the stairs one step at a time was easier, though still labour intensive.

He slowly heaved on his padded wax jacket, ensuring all fastenings were secure to stop the chill wind from getting in. Opening the door, he found Jess waiting, though as soon as she saw him, she ran off. Looking up, Arthur saw the early rays of light shining over the barn roof. Feeling slightly disoriented, he closed his eyes and turned his head from side to side, slowly stretching his neck. Still feeling uneasy but unsure why, he shrugged the thought to the back of his mind and went to look for Jess.

Approaching the paddock, he caught sight of Toby stretching his neck over the fence and gingerly selecting an apple from the nearest bough. With a sharp tug, he was eagerly enjoying the fruits of his labour.

As Arthur stumbled closer, he could make out the figures of Bessie and Maisie as they left the byre together in the growing sunrise. "I haven't already seen to the cows, have I?" he muttered under his breath, confused, placing a hand on his forehead as though the touch would bring back the recollection of his actions.

A wave of knotted dread spread throughout his bones, and his gut was pitted with horror. Turning sharply, grabbing the fence to steady himself, he squinted his eyes to peer ahead across the chicken coop and goose huts. The chickens were just starting to appear from their hen houses but, the geese were a different matter. The doors were still open, and scattered across the field were white and grey bumps of feathered masses.

Jess was padding through the field, sniffing intently everywhere she could; she followed the scent to the hedgerow;

seemingly, the trail ran cold there. She looked back over her shoulder and, seeing Arthur, she walked up slowly to him, head hung low and looking dejected.

His eyes welled with tears, vision blurry, his knees folded as he sank to the ground. A curled ball of devastation, frustration and grief intermingled with wracking physical pain. He screamed curses into the ground, berating himself and his life; he screamed until his lungs burned.

Eventually, in more pain than he ever thought possible and the insatiable need he had to move, he raised his forehead from the grass and shuffled himself to sit leaning against a fence post. His legs straight out in front of him, he threw his head back against the post with a dull thud, staring at the sky above as the scarlet waves against the golden clouds were illuminated by the developing sunrise.

Rolling his eyes to the side, he saw Jess stood staring at him, tail between her legs and ears back. "Come here," he uttered hoarsely. "I know it wasn't your fault, Jess; it's completely mine."

She padded slowly up to him, her eyes anxiously watching. He reached out his worn hand and rested it on her head.

"It's all my fault." He choked back more tears as he tried to smile weakly at Jess.

She licked his face and sat beside him.

His hand fell slowly down her back, pulling her a little closer to him. "Jess, we're not going to sleep until each and every one is put away tonight."

6

Sometime later, after summoning the strength to haul himself back up off the cold, hard ground, Arthur inspected the extent of the damage. The fox had managed to kill about two-thirds of his gaggle, beheading or at least snapping their necks. It wasn't the first time he had seen a massacre, but he had hoped he'd seen his last. The worst part was always the casualties that were another consequence of an attack like this; he had to humanely kill almost half of the remaining geese as they were so traumatised, that was if they didn't die before he could help them.

The few surviving geese were seemingly the only ones who had the common sense to take themselves into their houses the night before, that or they were the fastest at escaping the exhausting fox. Arthur had spent time with each one, in turn, examining for any wounds or signs out of the ordinary. He made sure to give them time to accept the ordeal, too; he could hear them repeatedly calling out for the deceased geese and hoped it wouldn't be long before they gave up.

Over the following week, Arthur doubled his efforts to ensure he stayed awake until all animals were safely away at night. He continued to take the tablets Harry had given him though they weren't much help in easing any of the symptoms. He was sure he'd double dosed a few times, forgetting whether he had already taken them; in all honesty, he couldn't really remember what day it was anymore. Jess was a blessing; she knew the routine and was becoming quite vocal at medicine times.

"I'm coming, I'm coming," Arthur muttered as he shuffled through the house towards the kitchen in answer to the beckoning tone of the phone. "Hello?"

"Arthur, it's Harry, sorry it's late. Someone has just replied about your ad for Toby. They're going to come over to have a look tomorrow."

"Tomorrow," Arthur mumbled, half-dazed, and scribbled down the word in his diary.

"Are you alright? Did you get that?"

"Tomorrow," Arthur replied, trying to sound confident.

"Alright, chap, I'll catch you later." Harry hung up the phone.

Arthur paused for a while before registering the dial tone; he placed the phone back on the receiver and glanced at the clock above the window. With a sigh, he pulled the blanket closer around himself and shuffled back to his sofa, Jess following at his heels. His fatigue levels were beyond debilitating, and he crashed amid a cocoon of blankets - another day where he couldn't face the stairs just to go to bed.

His sleep was restless and full of dreams. He was standing in a field, the sky darkening before the storm; he cried encouragement out to Toby as he tried to push the old plough through the sod. Obedient and determined, Toby continued to pull, and Arthur followed behind him, the freshly inverted soil trailing in their wake. The rain was beginning to fall; Arthur urged Toby to keep going, just until they finished the field. There wasn't far to go.

The wind whipped the rain into his face, stinging his cheeks and making it hard to see. More than once, he tripped, catching the plough to steady himself. He continued to trudge forward. He could feel the plough slipping, which made him more determined to finish the row.

As soon as they were finished, Arthur praised Toby, turning to admire their field of hard work. The field was flat and covered in grass, with no neat rows ready for planting. Arthur, in shock, turned back to Toby; he wasn't there, "Toby? Toby!"

"Arthur?" a gentle firm hand touched his shoulder, "Arthur, are you alright?"

"Who…?" Arthur blinked, trying to disperse the remnants of tears. "Oh, Harry." He winced as he sat up. "What are you doing here?"

"I spoke to you last night," Harry remarked, clearly concerned.

"Last night?"

"Yes, about Toby."

"Toby? Is he alright?"

Harry shook his head slowly, "Toby's fine; it's you I'm worried about. The couple turned up to look at him and couldn't find anyone to talk to. They called me to find out what was going on. I was worried and came over straight away, letting myself in with the spare key. I tell you, Jess was relieved I turned up. How long have you been like this?"

"Like what?"

"Holed up, dead to the world on the sofa?"

"I don't know… what time is it?"

"Four o'clock roughly."

"What are they doing coming here at that time in the morning?"

"It's afternoon," Harry sighed. "Are the tablets not helping?"

Arthur grumbled, trying to escape from the blankets still clinging to him. He eventually stood, dragging his feet in small steps to the kitchen. Reaching into a cupboard, he pulled out the tablet box, Harry glancing over his shoulder to see.

"Arthur! You haven't taken any today at all!" Harry exclaimed. "And you've missed some in the week too."

"Ah, Doc, back off; I take them when I can."

"That's not good enough!" Harry glared.

"I don't need a doctor berating me," Arthur snapped.

"I'm concerned as your friend, not your doctor," Harry lamented.

"I'm sorry." Arthur hung his head, alternating his weight between his feet in an attempt to ease the pain.

Harry sighed, leaning against the kitchen work surface, arms folded. He watched as Arthur struggled to take the tablet dose out of the package.

"Is there someone who can help you?"

"Like a nurse or carer? No!"

"I mean family, what about Dan?"

"That useless brat?" Arthur swallowed the tablets, "I don't even know where he is. I lost track at least ten years ago," he added sorrowfully.

Looking at the open diary on the side, Arthur noticed the word 'tomorrow' scratched on the page. "Why did I write that?" he thought aloud.

"Because the people who wanted to see Toby came today," Harry reminded gently.

"Toby? Oh, do they want him?" Arthur sounded hesitant.

"No, they saw him out in the field, and I think his size put them off. You'd think people would at least do a little research before coming out to see an animal."

"I see," Arthur smiled to himself, almost relieved at the answer, though a deep vein of worry ran within him.

"What about a walking stick?" Harry's voice interjected his thoughts.

"What now?"

"I said what about a walking stick?"

"What for?" Arthur replied indignantly.

"I just thought that walking around would be a little easier for you that way. I mean, out here, no one sees you anyway if you're worried about looking old."

"I am old!"

"Then what's the problem?"

Arthur considered the possibility for a moment, "I think I might still have my father's."

"Well then, that's a start. Where is it?"

"Think I kept it beside the gun cabinet," Arthur remarked as he headed into the study, "Here it is."

"It suits you," Harry chuckled, "in any case, try using it and see if it helps at least a little."

"Yes, Sir."

A scratching at the door made them both turn; upon Harry opening it, Jess trotted through.

"Wondered where you'd gone," Arthur patted her head, "what do you think, girl?" Jess barked with a large wag of her tail.

"I think she approves," Harry laughed, "she probably wants to know why you didn't think of it sooner, especially since it was so close to hand."

"Because I didn't think of it," Arthur quipped back. "I don't suppose you'll help me with sorting the livestock out."

"Thought you'd never ask. It's been a while since I helped out," Harry grinned as he rolled his sleeves up to his elbows, "just point the way, Arthur, old chap."

"Any more of this 'old chap' business, and I'll hit you with this stick," Arthur retorted.

Jess barked in agreement, wagging her tail as she followed them back outside into the chill autumn evening.

7

It was beginning to snow. The weather had been threatening this for the last week; nonetheless, Arthur had hoped it would stay away long enough for the Christmas orders to be fulfilled. It had taken several phone calls to try and explain why he wouldn't be able to supply geese this year and, indeed, every year going onwards. A lot of disgruntled and concerned customers slowly nibbled away at his heart before he became disconnected and unemotional about the situation.

The chickens were popular as usual, and due to the geese shortage, there was even more of a demand. Within the first hour of the customers driving up, he and Jess had worked out a system for boxing up the chickens, though he was somewhat grateful when people noticed the walking stick and offered to help out.

He was also appreciative of the fact that most, if not all of his customers were regulars from the local village and surrounding areas. He had John Tailor, the local butcher, to thank for that; he was an award-winning butcher who had gained quite a following and had the social network of an ant. It wasn't just his ability to communicate with others that was impressive, but also his knack for being able to organise such large groups seemingly effortlessly, like a well-oiled machine. He and Harry helped Arthur advertise and sell his birds every year. Of course, John was supplied with a large quantity of birds for his shop too and was no stranger to preparing them. It had been a system that ran smoothly for a long time, at least twenty-five years.

Finally, the last hen was sold. Arthur hung a 'Sold Out' sign on the gate. He looked over the coop again in sad remembrance of the fact that he wouldn't be restocking. The empty hen houses stood, resembling an old ghost town with dust and tumbleweed, like those he had seen in spaghetti westerns.

Hobbling, he began making his way back to the farmhouse. He glanced at the other field where the geese used to be. The ones that had survived the attack he had given in thanks to those that had helped him; Harry, of course, was number one on that list. He sighed. It was like looking at an unmarked grave; no evidence life had existed there apart from the houses that stood as lonely headstones. A reminder of the way of life he was leaving behind.

The only birdlife left was the ducks. They had always been just a hobby and were relatively easy to take care of. A small, solemn smile graced his lips at the thought of how much longer he could indulge such a hobby. Their soft quacks were almost as endearing to him as Jess's tail wagging when he spoke to her.

Entering the barn, he grabbed a bucket and threw in a scoop of oats. Then, grabbing as big an armful of hay as he could, he made his way to the stable. Toby was pleased to see him, whickering as he saw the figure approaching him from across the courtyard through the snowfall.

No one else had approached, looking to give Toby a new home. Arthur's concern grew daily as he worried about how much longer he could look after him before either one of them got sick.

"What you thinking about?" Harry called from the kitchen door.

"Not much," Arthur gave Toby a quick pat and tottered over to the farmhouse, his feet numb even through the thick-lined boots. "Were the ladies alright?"

"Bessie was a sweetheart as usual; Maisie was a bit temperamental, but we got the job done. I left the churns in the barn for you," Harry beamed as he stood back to let Arthur in.

Arthur paused to swap from boots to his slippers. He considered exchanging his coat for his blanket but decided that he was so cold he would use both instead. A small voice moaned at the back of his mind, reminding him that this wasn't normal for him: someone who embraced all weathers. He folded into a chair at the kitchen table as Harry brought over a cup of tea, a warming smell of stew filling the room.

"Have you thought of using a wheelchair or, better yet, a mobility scooter?" Harry suddenly asked.

"No," Arthur raised an eyebrow at his friend, "and I don't want to, either."

"Just hear me out. Now that you haven't got the feathery fiends out there, you should focus on not pushing yourself; you could still do the milking without issue."

"It isn't happening, Hal," Arthur glared.

"Well, why not?"

"Because it's a nuisance. I don't need to go to the fields to work, so I can easily drive to the ducks and back if need be. Everything else is in the courtyard. It's too much effort to get in and out of a blooming chair without trying to do work as well. The stick is more than suitable."

"But-"

"It isn't happening!" Arthur slammed his empty mug back on the table.

Harry scrutinised Arthur's face before, with a resolute slap on his knees, he stood up to dish out the stew. He placed the steaming bowls on the table before adding thick, crusted bread and a still mostly unspreadable butter between them.

"Since when did you know how to cook?" Arthur commented, eager to change the subject.

"Since I knew I was going to be helping you today," Harry chortled, fighting the butter with a knife.

"Maybe I should get you around here more often."

"Only if you want stew!"

The two continued to chat over dinner. Jess lay happily on the floor in front of the oven, chewing on a knuckle joint - a treat from John - in between her paws.

It wasn't long before Harry disappeared home with a goose under his arm to give to Jeannie. Arthur locked the door after his friend and turned to Jess. "Well then, time for bed, what say you?"

Jess wagged her tail, and with a short bark, padded her way to the stairs. Arthur looked down at her with a hesitant grin. "Alright, you win; let's go upstairs."

It was a slow climb; he was exhausted, and with each step, he considered just staying there for the night. Jess, on the other hand, had a different idea and barked from behind him in encouragement to keep going. Finally, they reached the top, and Arthur was more than glad when he could slip in between the sheets and the mountain of blankets to sleep.

Before he turned off the light, he watched Jess going round in circles before settling on the rug. "You know if Mary ever found out you were up here, there would be hell to pay for the both of us."

Jess's big brown eyes watched him, her eyebrows raised as she looked up from the floor.

"You're a good girl, Jess. I don't know what I'd do without you."

Her tail thumped slowly against the floor as it wagged in appreciation.

"Good night, Jess," he saw her lower her eyes, and he turned out the bedside light.

8

The snow was piling up thickly on the window sill, and the long stretches of empty fields were buried, the redundant birdhouses just barely visible in the distance. Dusk was falling as Arthur gazed lazily out of the window from his armchair. Just watching the snowflakes drifting to the ground sent icy shivers throughout his body.

Jess was asleep on the rug; she had moved away from the fire and now lay with her nose not far from Arthur's foot. Every now and then, her ears would twitch when Arthur shifted himself in his seat or rubbed his legs. She had even looked up a couple of times when he had murmured and groaned.

Arthur had a book in his gloved hands, but he hadn't turned the page for a very long time. He had reread the same passage at least four times, and even though he knew he had followed the words, he was struggling to comprehend any meaning from them. He lowered his arm, resting the book upon his knee, his thumb wedged between the pages as a bookmark.

A knock at the front door had Jess standing within seconds. She stretched her back with a big yawn as Arthur, grumbling, opened the book again and balanced it face down on the arm of the chair. He slowly dragged himself out of the seat, picked up his walking stick he had rested against the desk and made his way to the kitchen.

"I'm coming," he yelled as there was another knock at the door. "Who could be knocking on farm doors at this time of night?" He muttered to Jess.

Opening the door, Arthur froze, squinting up into the face before him. "Who are you?" He asked cautiously; Jess sniffed around the stranger's legs.

"You don't remember?"

"I know all the faces I need to know, and yours isn't one of them," Arthur replied, disgruntled, having struggled to get up for this nonsense. "If you're selling something, I don't have the money for it. If you're buying, you're too late. I have no stock left. Should've come before Christmas."

Arthur went to shut the door, his whole body screaming to get out of the cold night air. The man blocked the door with his foot and pushed the door open again with his hand.

"Oi!" Arthur lost his balance and stumbled a couple of steps back, "I'm warning you." He brandished his stick in the air shakily. Jess growled, her hackles up and teeth bared.

"Sorry, Dad," the stranger apologised, backing up and taking his hand off the door. "I didn't think I would knock you over."

"Dad?" Arthur felt a stabbing pain in his chest. "What kind of cruel joke are you trying to play on an old man?" he whispered, lowering his stick. "I don't know what you think you're playing at, but it's a sick joke. Now get out of here before I call the police!" He yelled, more determined.

"Dad, come on, it's me – Daniel," the stranger pleaded. "Look I know it's been a while, but it really is me! I can prove it! I left when I was sixteen after we had a fight-"

"Everyone in the village knows that!" Arthur interrupted, desperate for the pain in his chest to subside; his head was starting to throb.

"Well…then… what about the time I accidentally left the pigsty gate open and the piglets escaped, and we spent the rest of the day chasing after them to round them up?"

The stranger paused for breath, his eyes searching and desperate, "I can tell you so many things if you still don't believe me."

"You better come in," Arthur replied flatly, "it's cold stood here. Jess, it's alright."

Jess stood back, she had stopped growling, but she remained wary of the newcomer, her eyes following his every move. Arthur shut the door and motioned for Dan to take a seat at the table. He flicked the switch on the kettle and carefully lifted two mugs from the cupboard. "So how have you been?"

"Alright, I guess," Dan replied quietly. He had run the conversation he was going to have with his dad over in his mind so many times on the way here but, now it was all for nought. He didn't know what to say, "what about you? How have you been?"

"I've been," Arthur answered, popping teabags into the mugs.

The awkward silence that followed hung between them, the only noise coming from the fire crackling in the study and the kettle boiling. Arthur sighed as he summoned up enough strength to lift the kettle. Shakily he poured the water before replacing the kettle with a thud. He placed the mugs on the table as controlled as he could before sitting down opposite his son, wrapping the blanket tighter around his shoulders.

"So why did you come back?" Arthur asked, unable to look his son in the eye.

"Was I not supposed to?" Dan stared into the mug between his fingers, "Dad, I'm sorry."

"What for? Leaving here or not sending a single word my way for the last nineteen years even just to tell me you were still alive?"

"Look, I know I was wrong-" Dan started, looking up at his father.

"What and sorry makes it all better?" Arthur snorted. "Or are you here for money?"

"What? No!" Dan reeled back in his chair. "I heard you were ill-"

"Ill? So, you think it's alright to turn up if I'm on my deathbed? I don't know what you've been told, but I don't want any pity, and there's no money to hand out."

"That's not why I'm here!" Dan snapped, the anger bubbling inside of him. "You were always like this. Always concerned about yourself and never what I had to say!"

"I've never cared about myself!"

"That's all you ever did! Ever since Mum died, it was always about you. If you were alright, then everyone else had to be too."

"You don't know what it was like for me!"

"She was my mum! Do you think I don't know how much it hurt to lose her?"

Arthur slammed his fist on the table. "Is this why you came back? To drag up the past?"

"Of course not!" Dan yelled back before quietly adding, "I have a family. Amelia, my wife, told me to come and make amends."

"Oh, so I am that bad you had to be told by your wife to see me? At least you listen to someone."

"That's not what I meant, I couldn't come back before, and I thought I had left it too late."

"Too late? Well then, are you happy with what you see? A frail old man who can't stand straight and can no longer work? Did you come for a laugh?" Arthur's cheeks were red with the emotions running hot under his skin. "Maybe you were better off not coming back after all."

Dan stood, pushing the mug away from the table's edge. "I know I was wrong back then. Heck, I know I was more trouble than I was worth, but at least I had a life!"

"Life? You wouldn't even have that without me but look at the way you treat your own father! A hissing goose gives more love and respect than you ever did!"

"Maybe this was a mistake after all," Dan stared, biting his lower lip. "I'm sorry to bother you."

Dan turned his back and banged the door shut behind him, his tea only half drunk. Jess crept up to Arthur and placed her head gently on his thigh, licking at the tears that fell on her nose.

9

It was cold in the car. Dan rested his arms across the top of the steering wheel, head pressed against them. He had considered calling Amelia but couldn't bring himself to bother finding his mobile; besides, he knew what she would say. She'd scold him for being the one who stormed out, and at least fifteen reasons would roll off her tongue as to why he should go back, though currently, he could think of only the reasons why he shouldn't. He closed his eyes in defeat.

Realising he couldn't stay in the car overnight, he reached into his pocket to fish out his mobile. In the light of the screen, he could see his breath clouding before his face. He searched for the nearest hotels, considering that a motorway services might be more readily available at this time of night. Slipping the phone into a holder on the dashboard, he pressed for directions. Fastening his seatbelt, he started the car and was soon on his way, heading back towards the village.

Even though it was dark and covered with a thick layer of snow, the village was exactly how he remembered it. Childhood memories burst forth into his mind with each twist in the road or building he recognised. Almost subconsciously, he paused opposite the village green, looking down the road to his left. With new resolution, he turned down this road and parked in front of the village doctors, the voice from his phone immediately asking for him to turn around.

Harry was just sitting down for dinner when the bell rang. "It's always the way," he huffed as he rose back out of his chair. "Won't be a moment, dear," he smiled with a wink at his wife as she continued to lay the table. He sauntered towards the front door, whistling, 'I Saw Three Ships.'

"Dan? Well, lad, you'd better come in," Harry stepped to one side welcomingly, yelling towards the kitchen. "We have one more for dinner, Jeannie."

"Oh?" a cheerful voice called back. "Who is it?" A plump figure bustled into the doorway, wiping her hands on a tea towel, peering over her glasses. "That can't be Arthur's boy, can it? Bless my soul! Dan Adley, get yourself in here!" She beckoned with open arms, wrapping Dan in a quick warm embrace in the hallway.

Harry shut the outer door with a soft click and ushered them all back towards the kitchen, rubbing his hands together to generate some heat from the chill that had crept in. Jeannie hurriedly placed another plate in the oven to warm up and lay an additional spot at the table. Dan took his seat gratefully though he felt embarrassed for imposing.

"I know that look," Jeannie smiled, "don't you worry about a thing. You know we've always had room for you here," she beamed at him before continuing to place the food on the table.

"We'd find room to house and feed an army if we needed to," Harry joked, gently elbowing Dan in the arm with a wink. Then quietly whispering, "I take it you went to see your father?"

Dan nodded in response.

Harry sighed and patted his shoulder in a comforting gesture. "We'll talk more about it after dinner," he promised, then more loudly added, "My dear, you have created an extravagant feast as always. What would I do without you?"

"Starve, most likely," she laughed, slotting spoons into the dishes on the table and sitting down herself.

Dinner with the Prior's was a welcome change after the day he had been through. It was hearty and familial; they always had been, even back when he was at school with their son Jack. Jeannie definitely hadn't lost her touch where cooking was concerned. She hadn't lost her voice either; she was delighted to regale the lives of everyone in the village to him. It was as if she was trying to catch him up to speed with everything he had missed during the time he had been away.

After dinner, Dan helped with the washing up, leaving Harry to dry and put away. Jeannie was most insistent that Dan stayed the night and disappeared to set up a bed in the spare room for him. Harry showed Dan into the living room, handing him a cup of tea and sitting opposite him.

After a while of him staring into the tea, Dan broke the silence. "Thank you."

"Whatever for, lad? You knew you were always welcome - even when you left."

"I guess the longer I was away, the harder it was to come back," Dan sighed to himself.

"And? Are you glad you did?"

"Yes, no, I don't know, really. He didn't even recognise me."

"I don't think I'd know my own son after nineteen years apart with no contact."

Dan looked up wistfully, "but you and Jeannie knew who I was; you even contacted me."

"Ah, you need to thank Jack for that," Harry sipped at his tea. "This social media thing isn't for me, but Jack, he's taken himself off to medical school and come back with computer skills. He's decided for himself that he wants to take over from me here when I retire, the fool." Harry chuckled. "I happened to say something about you, and he was on it straight away. Somehow, through that gadget of his he calls a phone, he managed to get hold of you for me."

"That makes sense," Dan rolled his eyes with a small smile. "Dad wasn't exactly forthcoming, though. Well, that's not what I mean. I wasn't expecting open arms or anything, but I guess I was hoping for more."

"Try looking at it from his point of view. His son ups and leaves after a fight and doesn't even send a postcard. Then, when he's stricken with a degenerative affliction, he has to face the fact that he is going to lose the only constant in his life, his family's farm. That's his way of life taken away from him. He's all on his own, and he faced it alone without ever asking anyone for help, not even me.

"Then, one night, his long-lost son returns. He's old and feeble and doesn't dare hope for a miracle. In all honesty, I believe he's scared. He doesn't want to let anyone else into his life just to lose them again, and he's convinced his illness will continue making him lose everything he cares about. Animal or human."

Dan wiped the back of his hand over his eyes, trying to stop any tears from forming. "I hadn't thought about that. I'm really a selfish guy."

"He cares about you a lot, Dan. He never stopped searching for you, trying to follow any leads he had on you, even if it was just village gossip. He was heartbroken when you left home. I'll tell you a secret," Harry confided, placing his cup down on the coffee table. "I've only seen your father drown his sorrows twice. The first was when your mother died, and the second was when you left. The day the last lead he followed on your whereabouts ended empty-handed, he gave up alcohol completely. He even stopped coming round for dinner. He completely shut down and devoted himself to the farm. That was about ten years ago now."

Dan placed his hand across his eyes to hide the tears as they welled uncontrollably. Harry watched sympathetically, realising that the nineteen years apart had been just as taxing on Dan as they had been on Arthur.

10

Dan was lying on his back, staring up at the beams in the ceiling from the bed Jeannie had prepared for him. He remembered the room well, although it had been decorated. It was Jack's old room; they had spent many a time talking and laughing the night away here. It was quiet now, though. So quiet that he was beginning to feel lonely.

Rolling on to his side, he glanced at his mobile on the bedside table. Hesitating, he took a deep breath before propping himself up against the pillows, reaching over and speed dialling Amelia. She answered within the first few rings, though he couldn't say anything, he didn't know what to say.

"Honey? Dan, hey, you haven't been like this since you were in the army and called because you missed me," Amelia's voice was soft.

"I do miss you," Dan replied quietly.

"Is everything okay?"

"I don't really know," Dan sighed.

"Where are you now?"

"Harry Prior's."

"Harry Prior? The man who contacted you?"

"Yes, he's the village doctor. I was friends with his son back in school. He's also Dad's best friend; they were each other's best man and things…"

"Did you go to see your dad?" Amelia asked cautiously.

"It didn't go well," Dan sounded regretful. "It's a long story."

"You got into a fight with him, didn't you?"

Dan remained silent.

"I was expecting you to. I don't think it would be normal if you two didn't clear the air after all these years."

"I guess you're right. But I walked away again; it was like my reasons for being there were never going to be good enough for him."

"But you feel bad about doing that now, don't you?"

He made an agreeable noise down the phone. His eyes were stinging; he pinched the top of his nose and sighed. "Harry filled me in on a lot of things that have happened... I didn't realise..."

"It's okay, honey, we say and do things when we're hurt, but it's only when we feel guilty for our actions that we can be held accountable and start to make amends."

"What if it's too late?" Dan asked, choking back his tears.

"It's never too late to take responsibility for our past mistakes."

Dan gave a watery smile, "Thank you."

"I don't know what you are thanking me for," Amelia gave a low laugh. "You know damn well you aren't coming back here without making amends with him." She paused before adding in a thoughtful whisper, "He's alive; you don't know how lucky you are before he's gone. Don't keep him waiting anymore."

"Babe, I'm sorry," Dan felt his chest tighten as he heard her soft sobs. It was coming up to a year since her father had been cruelly taken away by cancer. He had been an influential role model for the both of them over the years, so much so that Amelia had been resolved to name their son after him without any compromise.

"I'm going back tomorrow," Dan tried to change the subject, hoping to take her mind off her own father. "Harry's going to come with me, act as peacemaker. I want to tell him about you, George and Maria. It would be good for them to have at least one grandparent... even just for a little while."

"Is his condition that bad?" Amelia sounded worried, though at least she wasn't crying anymore.

"Harry explained some of it to me, essentially Myalgic Enceph...whatever, ME... it's horrible and debilitating. He's already reduced a vast majority of his livestock, but to be honest, I don't know how much longer he can pay for himself."

"Why doesn't he come and live with us?"

Dan snorted involuntarily. "He wouldn't do that. The farm has been in our family for generations, and it's all he has ever known. He's a stubborn old fool, but even I wouldn't change him."

"Then how about we move to the farm?"

"What?"

"It would mean that he doesn't have to leave his home, and we would be there to help him. He could teach you the tricks of the trade, as it were. Besides, I know you have never really been satisfied with carpentry like my father. George and Maria would love it!"

"Well, he does have a gorgeous Collie called Jess; Maria would be all over her," Dan mused before contributing in a serious tone. "But what about your work? A school for George? The cost of moving and trying to save the farm? In any case, Dad would never agree to it. There's too much heartache between us for me to turn around, take charge and move us all there."

"It's fine, honey," Amelia's voice was infectiously optimistic. "We have money from my Dad, and we could sell here or even rent it for a while before we sell. I can organise a school for George and who doesn't need a vet? I'll find work closer to the farm."

"Don't get ahead of yourself." Although he was smiling, he was trying to ground her thoughts before she got carried away. "I don't even know if Dad will see me again-"

"He will," Amelia interrupted.

"Millie, I'm being serious. I don't know what Dad is thinking on the matter, and I'm not going to force the issue. This is a big decision for him too; you can't make it for him."

"I know, but at least you know it's an option. I'm more than happy to leave it open but, just remember, I'm more than happy to support this."

Dan smiled; he knew she couldn't see him but it didn't stop him. She always found a way to make life positive and was always so optimistic about challenges, "I love you."

"I love you more, you idiot."

11

It had stopped snowing by the time morning came around, sunlight glistening across the snow that was blanketing the ground. Harry and Dan were in Harry's Land Rover as it handled the fresh falling of deep snow better than Dan's little city car. Jeannie had made sure that they both had breakfast before they left, and she packed extra for them to give to Arthur.

The conversation was light, Harry mostly talking about his son Jack and how Dan really should see him before he goes back home. Although Dan was listening and he gave his input at the relevant times, his thoughts were occupied with the idea of moving to the farm with his family, how Arthur might react and all the things he was starting to hope he could do there.

It wasn't long before they were in the courtyard of Adley's Farm. Trudging through the snow, they reached the front door, knocked and stood waiting in the cold wind. Jess barked in greeting and ran over to them from the barn. Harry and Dan shared a quick glance at each other and started to head across the courtyard, just as Arthur appeared in the barn doorway.

"What are you doing over here?" Harry asked worriedly.

"I couldn't sleep," Arthur's eyes looked dark, his face gaunt and his complexion ashen. "I stripped it down and cleaned it."

"Stripped what down?" Harry looked like he was about to explode. "What are you doing out here in this bloody weather?

Normally, when people can't sleep, they read a book or watch television!"

"I'm obviously not normal."

"No, you're downright ridiculous. This isn't going to help you one bit!"

Arthur took a while to respond, his eyes struggling to stay open. "My mind wouldn't stop."

"Are you telling me you have been awake all night?"

"It isn't a problem," Arthur mumbled, trying to wave the issue aside.

"Of course it's a problem! Haven't I emphasized enough to you that you need to get into a routine and look after yourself? The only purpose this is going to serve, is you crashing for several days straight!"

Arthur huffed, knowing he was defeated. Admittedly, this was more due to the sheer fatigue that had him in its grasp than Harry's persuasive and stern opinions.

Dan had remained silent, watching the altercation between the old friends, his hands stuffed in his jeans pockets to keep them warm. It hadn't gone unnoticed, the vast change in Arthur since yesterday. His voice sounded gravelly and sore; his speech was slower and more monotone, not to mention the cacophony of moans and groans that had issued out of him in the short time since their arrival.

Harry caught and led Arthur by the arm back into the farmhouse, spurred on by the stifled coughs uttered from Arthur's lips. Dan followed, making sure Jess was in before shutting the door. It wasn't long before Harry had made them all a cup of tea, and they were sat around the table; Arthur huddled under a blanket.

"Dad, what were you doing in the barn?" Dan asked cautiously. Somewhere in his mind, he was expecting to be yelled at again. He was surprised to find that Arthur couldn't even look him in the eye.

"I couldn't sleep, couldn't read, so I decided to strip down the mower and prepare it ready for spring. I had a couple of Tilley lamps out there. Jess kept me company."

"Jess would keep you company if you were running starkers across the field," Harry mumbled under his breath.

"Dan... my boy." Arthur's eyes glazed over as he spoke, the excruciating physical aches of fatigue had finally caught up with him. "I'm sorry."

"It's alright, Dad, please don't be sorry." Dan's voice cracked as he held back threatening tears.

"You need to sleep," Harry announced, clearly concerned. "We can manage the animals, just rest, you old fool."

Arthur nodded slowly; it was too much effort to try and speak any more. His head felt hot and heavy, his stomach nauseous, and he was beyond exhausted, which came hand in hand with the shivers. Slowly screeching the chair back across the tiles, he leaned profoundly against the table for support as he willed his legs to hold him long enough to make it to the sofa.

Without hesitation, Dan was on his feet. He scooped his father into his arms, blanket and all.

"I'm not going to stand by watching you struggle."

He turned to the door and found Harry already there holding it open and Jess, wagging her tail, with the expectation of escorting them. In no time at all, they had Arthur in his room, tucked into his own bed. Harry shut the curtains and disappeared back downstairs though Jess refused to go even when he called her.

"It's alright, Harry," Dan called after him. "She can stay here with Dad; it's what she's used to, after all." He stood and let Jess take his place beside the bed, curling herself into a neat ball.

"Dan," Arthur's voice sounded weak.

"Just sleep for now Dad, I won't leave. I'll look after the animals for you, so don't worry."

"No… Dan…" Arthur's hand was shaking, but he still held it out, trying to find his son.

"I'm here," Dan consoled him as he went round to the other side of the bed and caught his hand. "I'm only going to be downstairs."

"No…" Arthur huffed.

"You don't want me to sort out the animals?" Dan questioned, confused.

"No… that's not what I meant." Arthur summoned all his energy to look Dan in his eyes, "I'm sorry."

Dan faltered, staring back at the weak greying eyes before him. "Whatever for…? Don't be silly. It's I who should be sorry. Well… I mean, I am, I'm sorry."

"I'm sorry, Dan," Arthur shook his head from side to side as his eyes began to water. "I'm sorry for not being there for you, for not listening-"

"Stop it," Dan whispered.

"I'm sorry… for not stopping you… when you left."

"Stop it, you old fool," Dan hushed, choking on his tears. "It's my fault, all my fault, but I'm here now. I'm sorry, Dad. I promise I'll make it up to you."

Arthur smiled weakly, feebly trying to squeeze the strong hand that held his. "Tell me about everything, I might fall asleep… but I really want to hear."

Taken aback, Dan felt a weight lift from his chest as he perched himself on the edge of the bed, a small smile gracing his mouth.

"Where do I start?"

"You said something about a wife… Amy… Emily…"

"Amelia. Yes, Amelia and two children, George and Maria. You're a Grandad."

"Maria…"

"Yes, after Mum."

"She would have liked that."

Dan grinned widely as the tears poured down his face. He told Arthur about joining the army and how he had met Amelia whilst on leave, though he left out the part that it was in a bar. He retold the tales of their wedding, trying his best to paint an image so clear that it was as though Arthur had always been there. He spoke of George, now four and just starting school and little Maria, who was enjoying her newfound freedom; now she was walking and talking to everything in sight.

Arthur closed his eyes, a faint smile clearly marked on his lips. Now and then, he gave small, breathy laughs in response, but it wasn't long before he fell asleep; soft wheezes escaped his weathered face and joined the snores from Jess by his side.

12

Disoriented from another night of unrefreshed sleep, Arthur slowly eased himself out of bed. Searching the room, he saw the late afternoon light creeping around the edges of the curtains. But no Jess. A chill rattled through his bones as hazy recollections from yesterday began to appear through the fog of his mind. Standing, he caught hold of the walking stick that was hanging precariously from the frame at the end of the bed and braved the stairs. At the bottom of the stairs, he could hear a voice softly whispering, and as he fully entered the kitchen, he could see Dan gently talking to Jess as he emptied food into her bowl.

"Dan?"

"Dad, good afternoon."

"I didn't think you'd still be here," Arthur replied, almost to himself, with a growing smile. "Afternoon, my boy."

"Do you want a cup of tea?" Dan asked, placing Jess's bowl on the floor and then flicking on the kettle.

"Please," Arthur sat down at the table. "What day is it?"

Dan placed the two mugs on the table and sat down himself. "Thursday, and here are your tablets."

Arthur nodded slowly to himself, desperately trying to focus his mind.

"Hey, I'm sorry to ask this," Dan began, "but do you have a spare jumper I can borrow? I managed to spill toothpaste down this one. I'd like to look at least a little bit respectable."

"I'm sure we can find something upstairs," Arthur commented, slowly massaging the cramping aches in his thighs for temporary relief.

After tea, tablets and a little attention from Jess, the two headed back upstairs. Arthur plonked himself down on the edge of the bed and motioned with a wave of his walking stick. "There should be jumpers on the shelves in there."

Dan made his way over to the large armoire standing against the wall; opening the doors, he found shelves of jumpers and trousers, ties were hanging on the inside of the door. There was also a hanging rack with a few shirts, dresses and skirts. Dan's first thought of surprise was regarding the women's clothing. His second was the realisation that he remembered the floral pattern on one of the dresses; it was his mother's.

Dan unhooked the hanger of the dress and pulled it gently out of the armoire. He turned to show Arthur, a questioning look plastered on his face.

"It was your mum's favourite dress," Arthur smiled solemnly. "I couldn't just throw it away."

"She's been gone a long time," Dan sighed, matter-of-factly.

"Well, I donated a lot. It was only the special ones I kept," Arthur sighed. "Then, after a while, I didn't need to open that side for the clothes I wanted, and it just slipped to the back of my mind. I knew they were there, but it wasn't a forefront thought anymore."

Dan sat down on the bed next to him. "I miss her."

"I'm surprised you remember her; you were only five."

"She used to be the one who collected me from school. It's pretty hard to forget the day Jeannie brought me home. She told Jack to stay in the car, and when we opened the door, you were sat here with Harry, drinking. I remember a bottle being on the table and the glass in your hand... you wouldn't look at me. Jeannie took me upstairs to grab some spare clothes, and then I was at the Prior's for at least a fortnight."

"We had just lost them," Arthur was shaking. "I didn't know how to tell you... I wasn't convinced myself."

Dan replaced the dress, paused and turned around to face his father. "Them?"

"I guess you were too little, too young to understand... you were going to be a big brother. But something went wrong." Arthur stood with the help of his walking stick and disappeared onto the landing, entering the door on his right.

Dan followed, curious and still slightly confused. The room smelled a little damp, and it was definitely colder than the rest of the house. The walls were half-decorated with wallpaper; the little that there was had started to peel. The window was bare and dusty - so much so that Arthur had to pull out his handkerchief and wipe the glass to be able to overlook the field below clearly. In the corner of the room stood an old-style wooden crib; it too was heavily dusty.

"She went into labour prematurely," Arthur reflected, staring out through the patch of window he had just cleaned. "The ambulance wouldn't get here in time. In any case, those were the days that an ambulance was basically a body moving vehicle: She would need to wait until she got to the hospital to be seen. Besides, they arrived too late anyway. I had called Harry, and he was here within ten minutes. He tried... he really did, but I appreciate it wasn't his area of expertise. Jeannie was here too... But it wasn't any good... she died in my arms. Not long afterwards, the ambulance turned up. The ambulance had just taken them away when Jeannie left to pick you boys up."

Dan found himself crying silently; he had never appreciated just how his mother had died; he only knew she was no longer there.

Arthur turned to face him, "I know I haven't been the best father to you; I struggled and threw myself into the farm. We had to eat and survive on an income somehow, and it was just harder with a small child in tow.

"I guess I knew all along, really. I was a bad parent to you, and I just didn't want to admit it. I can't describe to you how guilty and yet how grateful I was to Harry and Jeannie stepping in to look after you as much as they did. I felt... I didn't deserve to be your father... not after what had happened.

"All the small fights seemed so massive at the time, and yet I couldn't bring myself to tell you why I acted the way I did. Why I didn't shout and try to explain myself. Why I let you yell at me... Why eventually I would just walk away, back to the jobs that needed doing around here... How could I tell you that I believed I deserved it all for failing you, for failing to protect those I care about?

"I'm ashamed to say it, even now," Arthur admitted, looking into Dan's eyes pleadingly, "but please believe me, after that last fight, when I returned from the field, and you weren't there... I searched for you straight away... I didn't stop until all the faintest rumours about you had disappeared... After that, I could only hope..." Arthur rubbed a hand across his eyes before taking a deep breath and carrying on. "I've hoped for so long... and then, I treated you the way I did when you were finally before me. I guess, even though I never stopped hoping, I didn't want you to see me like this..."

"No one can blame you for what you did-" Dan stopped himself. "Well, apart from me... I didn't understand, though. You never told me..."

"What was there to tell a sixteen-year-old who hated the world he lived in? I wasn't about to add fuel to the fire and let you hate your mum too." Arthur placed a hand on Dan's shoulder before leaving the room.

Arthur hobbled his way to the other side of the landing and opened the door, standing to one side to let Dan go in first.

"It hasn't changed at all!" Dan exclaimed, starting to touch the furniture reminiscently. "No way, look at the TV! It's ancient!" He sat down at the pine desk that was mostly taken up by the television set. He stared incredulously around him. The walls were covered with posters, and the single bed was pressed against the wall in the corner. There was another chair beside the desk that had become home to a dusty rugby ball.

Arthur was stood in the doorway, leaning against the door frame. "I haven't touched a thing. I left it hoping you would come back."

"Nineteen years too late," Dan smiled remorsefully. "Hey, Dad?"

"What's up, boy?" Arthur smiled back, remembering how most of their conversations had always started like this.

"What if Amelia and I moved here to run the farm for you?"

Arthur stared wide-eyed. "What would you want to do that for?"

"To help you and give George and Maria a proper childhood. I mean, with a little remodelling, I could split this room in two for them and Amelia and I can redecorate the nursery."

"It's an awfully big undertaking…" Arthur was struggling to process the proposition. "You can't easily go on holiday, and it's hard work; the animals always have to come first. And what about Amelia? She can't just up and leave her job for this rundown farm-"

"It was her idea," Dan chuckled. "She said that we have no ties. The children would have a grandparent in their life, and besides, she's a vet. Living on a farm is her biggest dream. Actually, her words were 'who doesn't need a vet?' and she is sort of right."

"It's such an inconvenience," Arthur replied quietly, a voice in the back of his mind desperately begging to say yes.

Dan moved to stand next to him, looking down slightly to look into his eyes. "Think about it, Dad. We are ready and more than willing. But it's an undertaking for you too. Having been on your own for so long then suddenly having a full-blown family? It's not going to be easy for any of us." Dan placed a reassuring hand on Arthur's arm. "I want to do it because I don't want to see you lose the family home. It's been in the family for generations, and you've managed it on your own for so long. It's your way of life, and it's always the place I've thought of as home, even if I was too stubborn to come back sooner. I can't believe, after all the fights we've had, that you are going to let this illness beat you out of your home. Our home."

Arthur's lip wobbled slightly, and his eyes were threatening to start stinging. He took a deep breath and wrapped his arms around his son in a loving embrace. "Yes!"

13

The sun was beaming down with a gentle warmth on the ground below. Arthur sat lazily in the sunshine on the bench in the courtyard. His walking stick rested against the bench beside him, and Jess lay at his feet, panting in the heat. Arthur had his sunglasses on and was slowly thumbing his way through a book.

"Grandad!" A chorus of excitable shouts yelled as small feet scampered towards him.

"Hello," Arthur closed his book and grinned at the two rosy faces looking up at him. "How was school today, lad?" He asked, tousling George's hair with a large hand and turned to his granddaughter. "Miss Maria," he greeted as he picked her up and kissed her cheek.

She giggled as he set her down on her feet again.

"We were learning about caterpillars today," George replied as he stroked Jess's head; she had sat up and was now trying to lick his face.

"Do you know what likes eating caterpillars?" Arthur asked, a twinkle in his eye.

"Cows?" little Maria chirped.

"No," Arthur chuckled and pressed her nose with the tip of his finger.

"You?" George giggled, pointing a cheeky finger at him.

"Oi!" Arthur tickled George in reply, who laughed loudly.

"I know, I know," George blurted out, looking at his sister; they both turned to Arthur, "Ducks!"

Arthur chuckled and started to stand up. "Who wants to go and feed the ducks?"

George and Maria both gave excitable yells and began running towards the pond; Jess sensing the excitement, barked and wagged her tail as she trotted beside Arthur.

"Hello, Arthur," Amelia crossed paths with him as he was leaving the courtyard; she kissed his cheek.

"Hello, my dear," Arthur smiled and looked down at the baby in the car seat she was carrying. "Hello, Artie." He stroked the sleeping infant's cheek. "Going to feed the ducks," he winked at Amelia as he began walking again.

"Do you know where Dan is?" Amelia called after him.

"He was milking the cows last time I saw him," Arthur yelled back with a wave of his hand.

Amelia waved back, and Arthur continued past the paddock. Toby plodded over to the fence with a soft whicker. Arthur produced a strong mint from his pocket and patted his nose affectionately.

"Come on, Grandad!" George and Maria roared as they ran in circles around him.

"I'm coming. Walk nicely now," he reminded them, looking ahead at the chicken and geese filled pastures, "you don't want to scare the birds."

He glanced back at the farmhouse with a soft smile. Dan had fixed the gutter himself and hadn't hesitated to call an old work colleague to help fix the rendering after he had pulled away the ivy. He had also sanded and repainted all the windows, not wasting a moment inside or out, whether structurally or animal wise. Dan had thrown himself completely into his new work and still found time to chat with his father in the evenings if he wasn't already asleep.

Amelia had taken great pride in reinstating the vegetable garden and never hesitated for a chance to encourage the children in spending time there, teaching them everything she was learning herself, even in managing the orchard. Every day was a learning day with her.

They reached the pond, and Arthur sat down on the bench Dan had placed there for him. George and Maria both climbed onto the bench and sat on either side of him.

Fishing in his pockets, he pulled out two small bags of grain. "It's not caterpillars, but they like it all the same." He gave a bag to each of them; their hands held out eagerly.

The ducks, recognising they had company, swam over and then gave little shakes that ended at their tails as they stood on dry land. Their quacks were chattering away as the children scattered food for them.

Jess crawled under the bench, her head on her paws between Arthur's feet.

He bent down and scratched behind her ear. "Good girl, Jess." He leaned back and smiled to himself. It wasn't every day he could enjoy time with his family. His body reminded him frequently that he would never be able to be without physical discomfort. That he would have days when he couldn't remember even the silliest of things and even the stuttering and shivers of his worst days were always a constant threat. But he had gained his son back; his family had grown, and the farm was flourishing. And best of all, they were home.

Myalgic Encephalomyelitis (ME)

ME has been recognised by the World Health Organisation (WHO) since 1969; currently, it is classified as a Chronic Neurological Disease.

Around 200,000 people in the UK and over 1 million in the USA have ME. It is estimated that 25% of these people are either bedbound or housebound.

The NHS clarifies symptoms as:

- Fatigue – Persistent and recurring, one recovers slowly after physical exertion.
- Insomnia – Sometimes can be hypersomnia, unrefreshed and disturbed sleep.
- Pain – Headaches, muscle pain without inflammation, painful lymph nodes
- Cognitive Dysfunction – Difficulty thinking, inability to concentrate, short-term memory loss/impairment. Difficulties in word-finding, planning, organising thoughts, information processing.
- Physical and mental exertion makes symptoms worse.
- Flu-like symptoms.
- Dizziness.
- Nausea.
- Unexplained Palpitations, which can lead to PoTS – Postural Tachycardia Syndrome.

There is no test to determine ME. It is a process of elimination. It can only be diagnosed after all possible causes for the symptoms and other diagnoses have been ruled out and when the current symptoms have lasted for a minimum of 4 months for an adult.

Although the character of Arthur is diagnosed with ME, his suffering symptoms are based on a collection amalgamated from those I have seen in person from three separate individuals. Please note that ME differs from person to person, and though similarities can be traced, there is no given or definite synopsis of this chronic disease.

With Adley's Farm, I hope to not only sow the seed of awareness, but I also endeavour to spark a learning curiosity in those who wish to know more. I implore you to understand that this chronic disease is debilitating and still so much is unknown for those suffering.

For more information, please look up the NHS website and ME Research UK. There are other groups and websites, too, but these two have been my go-to for information other than my diagnosed volunteers.

Printed in Great Britain
by Amazon